MARTHA SPEAKS®

Martha's Nose for News

Adaptation by Jamie White

Based on TV series teleplays written by Ken Scarborough

Based on characters created by Susan Meddaugh

HOUGHTON MIFFLIN HARCOURT

Boston • New York

For information about permission to reproduce selections from this book, write to Permissions, Houghton Mifflin Harcourt Publishing Company, 215 Park Avenue South, New York, New York 10003.

ISBN: 978-0-544-13567-3 hardcover
ISBN: 978-0-544-08572-5 paperback

Design by Bill Smith Group
www.hmhbooks.com
www.marthathetalkingdog.com
Manufactured in China
SCP 10 9 8 7 6 5 4 3 2 1
4500420094

EXTRA! EXTRA!

Read all about it! I, Martha the talking dog, have become a newspaper reporter. I will now prove it to you by interviewing a well-known personality . . . Me!

Q. Martha, how did you learn to talk?

A. Excellent question, Martha. Ever since Helen fed me her alphabet soup, I've been able to speak. And speak and speak . . . No one's sure how or why, but the letters in the soup traveled up to my brain instead of down to my

belly. Now as long as I eat my daily bowl of alphabet soup, I can talk.

Q. And who do you talk to the most?

A. To my family—Helen, baby Jake, Mom, Dad, and Skits, who only speaks Dog. To Helen's friends—T.D., Alice, and Truman. To her cousin, Carolina. Oh, and to the people who take my order at Burger Boy. I love those guys.

Q. Why do humans love a talking dog?

A. What's not to love? Although sometimes they wish I didn't talk *quite* so much. My mouth caused big trouble when I first reported stories for Carolina's newspaper, *Carolina's Town Crier.*

Q. Oh, yes. Will you tell us what happened?

A. Now, that story could fill a book! But here's the scoop. It all started when Carolina received a strange machine . . .

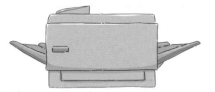

THE MONSTER IN CAROLINA'S ROOM

"Ta-da!" said Carolina.

She whipped a sheet off her dresser to reveal a box-shaped object. Helen, Alice, and Truman *ooh*ed and *aah*ed.

"Whoa!" said T.D. "You've got your own copy machine?"

Carolina nodded. "My dad got the newer model, so he said I could have his old one."

What's a copy machine? I wondered, sniffing it.

Carolina pressed a button. Suddenly, the thing made a loud WHIRR noise and sheets of paper whipped out of it.

"AAAH! IT'S ALIVE!" I shouted, jumping back.

Skits and I growled at the paper-spitting monster. "WATCH OUT!" I warned everyone.

Helen smiled. "Dogs aren't big on technology," she said.

Carolina pressed another button and the machine stopped.

"Wow," said Alice. "Imagine all the neat things you can do with this."

T.D. tried it out. He put his hand under the cover and made a copy of his palm. Then Alice copied her shoes. Even Skits used it. He made a copy of his new bone.

Soon we all lay on the floor, laughing at copies of tails, hands, and paws.

"Now what?" T.D. asked.

Carolina gathered the copies and flipped the pages like a book. "I've got an idea!" she said, hopping to her feet. "I'll make a newspaper!"

"A newspaper?" said T.D.

"Yes," she said. "For the neighborhood. I'll call it *Carolina's Town Crier.*"

She told us more about it on the way to the park.

"I'll need a team of ace reporters to sniff out the news," she said.

"Ooo! Skits and I can do that," I said. "We're great sniffers."

As proof, Skits gave her his freshly dug-up bone.

Carolina wrinkled her nose. "A dog reporter?" she scoffed, tossing the bone aside. "You've got to be kidding."

"No, really!" I said. "In the past three blocks, we sniffed out a half a dinner roll and a piece of lint-covered butterscotch candy."

"That's not news," said Carolina. "That's garbage. I need a scoop."

"A scoop?" I asked. "You want us to sniff out ice cream?"

"Not an ice cream scoop," said Helen. "When Carolina says she wants a scoop, she means a news story no one else knows about."

"Exactly," said Carolina. "Something sensational that makes a great headline. 'Dog

Bites Man' is not a scoop. 'Man Bites Dog'— now, that's a scoop."

I winced. "That sounds like an awful story."

"You're right," said Carolina. "It's been done. 'Man Bites Man Who Bit Dog' would be much better."

Ouch. With all these stories about biting, it's no wonder she's calling her paper Carolina's Town Crier, *I thought.*

SUPER SUCKER SCOOP

On the way to the park, we stopped at the yogurt shop. Helen bought the gang some Granny Flo Super Suckers while Carolina sat down to examine the *Wagstaff City Weekly*.

"We'll print our first edition on Friday," said Carolina. "Who wants to do what?"

"I'll cover arts and entertainment," Helen volunteered, grabbing that section from Carolina.

Alice took a section too. "I'll cover sports."

"And I'll make the crossword puzzle," said Truman, pulling the last of the paper from Carolina's hands.

She made a face. "Why don't you do a fun puzzle like connect the dots?"

Carolina took Truman's pen and newspaper from him and began working on the connect-the-dots puzzle.

"Where's the challenge in that?" he asked.

"Who cares?" she said. "When you're done, you've got a cute picture to hang on your fridge. See?" She held up her picture of a dopey walrus.

"Hmph," grunted Truman.

Before things got heated, we moved on to the playground. It always has the best trash can treats. Skits and I sniffed around, listening to the kids talk on the swings.

"T.D., what kind of news are you going to cover?" Helen asked, swinging.

He stood next to her, unwrapping his lollipop. "Something that will use my keen powers of observation," he replied.

"Science?" Helen asked.

T.D. looked around. "Even better," he whispered. "I'm going to be an investigative reporter."

"What do they do?" Alice asked.

"Investigate things!" he cried, raising his Super Sucker into the air like a superhero.

"Investigate?" I asked.

T.D. nodded. "It's when you dig around to find out what's *really* going on."

"See? I could so be a reporter," I said. "I'm always digging around. In fact, I'm going to do some right now." My sniffer had just caught a whiff of a bone buried beneath my paws—and by the smell of it, it was GIGANTIC!

"It's an expression," Helen explained. "Both *dig around* and *investigate* mean trying to find out more about something."

"Well, I want to investigate this smell," I said, digging with Skits. "I think there could be a story here."

"Who wants to read about smells?" Carolina asked. "While we're at it, why don't we write about what the neighbors have in their garbage, and where you can find dead stuff to roll in?"

I drooled. "Sounds like a real page-turner. I'm hanging on every word."

"I'm not going to print a story about a bone in my first edition," said Carolina. "A bone is NOT news."

"What are you going to investigate?" Truman asked T.D.

"I don't know," he said. "I need a story to grab people. Some secret everyone really wants to know."

Helen bit into her lollipop with a *CRUNCH*. "Well, I've always wanted to know how Granny Flo gets the bubblegum into her Super Suckers."

"That's it!" T.D. exclaimed. He grabbed the half-eaten sucker out of Helen's hand. "That's my scoop!"

"But how will
you get Granny to
tell?" Truman asked.
"Corporations don't
like to give out their
secret information."

"Easy," said T.D.
"I'll sneak into her
factory."

Then he told
us his plan.

T.D. GETS THE SCOOP

It was a stormy night when T.D. biked to Granny Flo's factory. Dressed in a trench coat and fedora, he tiptoed inside, taking photos. Nothing was going to stop him from getting the scoop of the century!

Little did he know that Granny was watching him on her office's secret monitors.

"It's that investigative reporter again," she said to herself. "Still trying to find out how I get the bubblegum into my Super Suckers. Well, if he wants that information, he'll have to catch me first."

With a leap, Granny flew out of her office and onto its balcony. Then—*whoosh!*—she slid down its spiral staircase to the factory floor. It looked like she was going to escape, when—

"Hold it, Granny!" ordered a voice from above.

Startled, she looked up to see T.D. on the balcony.

"The people have a right to know," he said.

"Sorry, sonny!" she snarled. "That's top-secret information."

Then Granny Flo was on the go again. T.D. jumped to the ground and took off after her on his skate shoes.

"Whoa!" he cried, picking up speed.

A few feet ahead, Granny hopped onto a moving conveyer belt. T.D. rolled alongside it, narrowly missing hanging lights and shelves of soup cans. He'd almost reached her when

Granny leapt to the ground and ran down a hallway.

"Take this!" she said, overturning a cart of laundry in T.D.'s path.

T.D. saw the obstacle, but he was going too fast to stop. It was either jump or crash.

"Aaah!" he cried, soaring over the cart. He landed, just as Granny got into a forklift and sped off. T.D. chased her, but he wasn't fast enough. She pressed a lever and the forklift raised her up onto another conveyer belt, which zoomed her toward an open window.

"So long, kid!" she called, stepping through it. Granny jogged across the roof, where a helicopter waited for her. As soon as she was inside, it lifted into the air.

"Can't catch me!" cackled Granny, looking out the window.

A familiar voice greeted her from the pilot's seat. Granny couldn't believe her ears.

"So," said T.D. "For the record, how *do* you get the bubblegum into the center of your Super Suckers?"

"Rats!" Granny scowled.

And that's how the amazing T.D. got the scoop and went on to become the best investigative reporter the world has ever known!

MYSTERY OF THE MISSING MUSTACHE

Okay, nothing in that last chapter really happened. It was T.D.'s fantasy. But it did make Carolina interested in his Super Sucker story.

"What're you sitting around for, T.D.?" she said. "Get that scoop!"

He took
off on his bike.
Skits and I ran
after him. (Not that

we were interested in the story.
We just like to chase things with wheels.)

When we got to Granny's factory, it was locked. A guard peered out at us from a small window in the door.

"We're from the press," said T.D. "We're here to research Super Suckers."

"Research?" she asked. "As in *study*?"

"Yes," said T.D. "We're here to learn about them. Just the facts, ma'am."

"The factory's in Alaska," snapped the guard. She slammed the window shut.

"Super Suckers aren't made here?!" T.D. cried. "Looks like my sucker scoop has hit a snag."

"Because it'd be impossible to ride your bike to Alaska?" I asked.

"No!" said T.D., getting back on his bike. "Because my mom would never let me miss that many days of school. I'll have to uncover another big story."

"Uncover? Like when you find out something secret or hidden?" I asked.

"Exactly."

"You can have the bone story I uncovered," I offered. "I can't write it. Dogs can't type."

"Thanks," said T.D. "But I think Carolina's right. A bone isn't really news." Then his eyes lit  up. "I've got it! The police! Maybe they've uncovered a story that's fit to print. Want to come?"

"No," I said. "Skits and I are going to work  on that bone. It may not be news, but it sure smells interesting."

Later that day, T.D. was leaving the police station just as I was running by it with a pack of my dog pals.

"Did you uncover a scoop yet?" I asked him.

"Nope," he sighed. More dogs ran past him. "Whoa! Where are they all going?"

"To the park," I replied. "They're going to help me dig up the bone. Want to come?"

"No," said T.D. "I'm still looking for information on a scoop-worthy story."

We didn't see each other again that day. But Helen, Alice, and Truman spotted T.D. while walking in the neighborhood.

"What's T.D. doing?" Truman asked, pointing to T.D.'s head popping up from behind some bushes.

They walked over to him. "Hey, T.D.!" Helen called.

"Shhh!" he said. "Do you want to blow my cover?"

"Are you doing some investigative reporting?" Alice whispered.

"Yes. See that guy?" T.D. asked. The kids peeked over the bushes at a man in a blue uniform. "I think he's up to something. I've seen him on this street before. Every day, it's the same thing. He walks up and down, up and down. He stops at all the doors. AND he's always got that bag with him."

Helen stood up. "He's a mailman! He *has* to walk this street every day. It's his route."

"He doesn't look like my mailman," said Truman. "My mailman has a mustache."

"Aha!" T.D. exclaimed. "Where's his mustache? He's a fake mailman!"

"He may not be a fake," said Alice. "Maybe someone stole his mustache."

"Another scoop!" said T.D., writing in his pad.

Helen snatched his pen. "That's not a scoop. There's more than one mailman in town and you know it."

"Maybe," said T.D. "But I think this guy's a fake. All I need to do is inspect his bag. You know, look closely at it."

"How are you going to do that?" asked Alice. "Won't he catch you?"

"Not if he's wearing finger handcuffs," said T.D., whipping some from his pocket.

Helen looked worried. "I've got a bad feeling about this," she said.

I DIG BONES

The next morning, T.D. made the front page of Wagstaff's paper. Only not in the way he'd hoped.

"'Local Boy Caught by Mailman's Bag'!?" Carolina hollered. In her room, the kids stared at a photo of T.D. in finger handcuffs. "T.D.! You were supposed to *get* the headline, not *be* the headline!"

Just then, Skits and I came in covered in dirt. "Hey!" I said. "Did you print the first edition yet? We've got a *big* story. Front-page stuff."

Carolina rubbed her forehead. "Tell me this is not about a bone."

"Uh, no, of course not," I said. "Tee hee. Well . . . sort of—yes."

"For the last time, let go of the bone!" said Carolina. "Nobody is interested in the bone!"

"You haven't seen it," I said. "It's enormous!"

"Agh!" Carolina groaned. She stormed out of the room, saying, "Helen, your dog has no nose for news."

"You guys want to see our bone?" I asked the others.

Alice shook her head.

"Um, I kind of agree with Carolina," said Helen.

"It doesn't sound like much of a story," said Truman.

They followed Carolina, leaving Skits and me with T.D. He moped on the bed.

"Did you find your scoop?" I asked him.

"No," he sighed. "I ended up being one instead. I'm a lousy investigative reporter."

"You want to see our bone?" I asked. "It's not news, but it might cheer you up."

T.D. shrugged. "Why not?"

Finally, a human agreed to see what we'd been digging up! I wondered what he'd think.

When we got there, T.D. gaped at what lay at the bottom of the hole. "JUMPING JUJUBES!" he cried, staring at the enormous bone.

"I know. Too bad it's not headline material," I said.

"Are you kidding?" T.D. said. "You've un-covered the biggest scoop this town has ever seen!"

A crowd gathered to see what the fuss was about. They called their friends and took pictures. Before long, news vans arrived too.

A reporter appeared next to me. "This just in," she said to a camera. "Two dogs investigating a smell today uncovered a large dinosaur bone. Scientists need to inspect further, but early observations indicate this is a very important find."

Meanwhile, Carolina watched the news with Helen, Alice, and Truman. "My scoop!" she wailed. "And I missed it!"

"Now," said the reporter, bending low so I could speak into her microphone, "let's hear about it straight from the pooch's mouth."

"No comment," I said. "I promised my story to another reporter."

"But don't worry, folks!" said T.D., jumping in front of the camera. "You can read all about it in the first edition of *Carolina's Town Crier.*"

Carolina gasped. Then she looked embarrassed. That day Carolina learned an age-old lesson: Never doubt a talking dog.

"So," said Helen, smiling, "I guess Martha has a nose for news after all."

CALL ME... ENCHILADA

Thanks to my scoop, the first edition of *Carolina's Town Crier* was a hit. A couple of days later, Helen and I decided to visit Carolina. We were on our way when we heard a scream.

NOOOOOO!

"Was that Carolina?" Helen asked.

"Sounds like trouble!" I said. "Come on!"

We ran as fast as we could. When Carolina opened her door, she looked miserable.

"Was that you who yelled?" Helen asked. "Are you okay?"

"No, cuz. I'm not okay," she said.

We followed her up to her room.

"Is your nose wet?" I asked. "If it's dry, you might be sick."

"That's only for dogs, Martha," said Helen.

"Oh, right," I said. "Did you try eating some grass?"

"I'm not sick," said Carolina. "I'm just upset. I don't have a single article for this week's *Town Crier.*"

"Is that all?" I asked.

"Is that *all?*" Carolina repeated. "Articles are the stories in newspapers and magazines. No articles, no newspaper!"

Helen sat on the bed. "There's a new snake exhibit at the zoo," she said.

"That's old news," said Carolina. "I need to sniff out my own stories."

"I could help you after soccer practice," Helen offered.

"That's too late," said Carolina. "My deadline is in a few hours."

"Aaah! *Dead*line!" I shivered. "That sounds scary."

"Believe me, it is," said Carolina.

"A deadline is the time when you need to be done with something," Helen explained.

"If I want my paper to be delivered tomorrow morning, then I have to type all my articles tonight by nine o'clock," said Carolina.

"Why nine?" asked Helen.

"Because that's when *International Icon* is on. Duh," said Carolina. "But it looks like I'm going to miss my deadline."

She collapsed onto her desk in despair. Helen rolled her eyes.

"I can help," I said.

Carolina looked doubtful. *"You?"*

"Why not?" I said. "Who found you the story about the dinosaur bone?"

"Martha has a point," said Helen.

"I'm a good listener," I said. "I heard you screaming from down the block. These legs were made for chasing moving objects *and* news stories. And . . ." I said, getting a whiff of Carolina's breath, "this nose can sniff out a hot tip like it can sniff out last night's enchiladas."

Carolina blushed and covered her mouth. "You really think you can get me some stories?"

"Mmmm . . ." I said, thinking about tortillas and meat and—

"She's still dreaming about enchiladas," Helen said.

"Look," said Carolina, kneeling next to me. "You get me a story I can type up before nine, and I'll get my dad to make you some of his famous enchiladas. How's that?"

"You'll have your story before your deadline, or my name isn't Enchilada!" I promised.

"You mean *Martha*," whispered Helen.

"Or my name isn't Martha!" I said.

DEADLINE DOGGIE

That evening, I hit the streets in search of stories.

I didn't get far before I heard the Parkingtons' dog, John, whining in his front yard. *Sounds like a story to me,* I thought.

"Hey, what's the news?" I asked him.

Ruff! Ruff!

"Really? Tell me more," I said.

I've known the Parkingtons for a dog's age, and I couldn't believe my ears!

Next I went
to Alice's house.
Her brother
Ronald's parrot
was squawking in
the window. I tried to
interview him.

"'This only works if you
don't repeat what I say," I said.

Squawk! "Repeat what I say."

"No, *don't* repeat," I said.

"*Don't* repeat."

Ugh. What a birdbrain.

Squawk! Squawk!

"Now you're talking. Tell me more," I said.

Then I followed my nose to a new pancake
restaurant. *I bet there's a story here,* I thought.
And, if I'm lucky, bacon.

I didn't find food, but I did find a chatty mouse with a hot tip.

At eight forty-five p.m., I reported my scoops to Carolina. Her smile grew as she typed them. "Wow! Wait until everyone reads this!" she exclaimed.

At nine o'clock, she printed her paper.

"We met our deadline!" she cheered. "You're my ace reporter. You're the best!"

I wagged my tail, thinking about tortilla-wrapped bundles of yum. "Now, about my salary . . ."

"One enchilada," she promised. "You just have to wait till the next time my dad makes them."

Sigh. I wished I'd set a deadline for getting that enchilada into my belly. A reporter's lot is not a filling one.

The next morning, T.D. delivered *Carolina's Town Crier* to our neighborhood. We thought everybody would love it. News flash: We were wrong.

GOSSIP HOUND

After breakfast, Skits and I took ourselves for a walk.

"It's not hard to find stories," I told him. "News articles are all around you, if you know where to look."

Just then, we heard shouting on Alice's porch. "You told Carolina about Commander Manly!" Ronald yelled.

"I didn't. Honest!" said Alice.

"Then how come I read about it on the front page of her paper? Who else could have told her?"

"I don't know," said Alice. "I didn't even know you still played with Commander Manly."

"I don't," said Ronald. "I just, uh, take him out of the box every now and then. It's a collector's item, okay?"

A boy and girl skipped past the house.

"Ronald and Commander Manly, friends for-e-e-ver!" they sang.

Ronald narrowed his eyes. "Carolina will pay for this!"

"Uh-oh. Time to go, Skits," I said.

We headed to Carolina's house. Mr. Parkington and Mr. Flapjack, the owner of the new restaurant, were talking to her on the porch. Loudly.

Mr. Parkington read from *Carolina's Town Crier:* "A birthday party for Mr. Parkington's sister, but guess who wasn't invited?" He looked at Carolina. "Of course, she wasn't invited. It was a surprise party!"

"A surprise party?" said Carolina.

"Yes!" fumed Mr. Parkington. "That's why my sister didn't get an invitation. We wanted to keep it a secret so that we could surprise her. Now the surprise is ruined."

"So a surprise is ruined. So what?" said Mr. Flapjack. "What about me?" He snatched the paper and skimmed it. "'Grand opening' . . . 'very exciting' . . . 'tasty food' . . ."

"Sounds great," said Mr. Parkington. "What's wrong with that?"

"I'm coming to it," said Mr. Flapjack, reading on. "'A great success, according to a

mouse named Chester, WHO LIVES IN THE RESTAURANT ALONG WITH HIS TWENTY RELATIVES'!" He shook the paper at Carolina. "Are you trying to put me out of business?"

"I said the food was tasty," said Carolina.

"TO MICE!" he shouted. "TO MICE! You said I had a restaurant full of mice!"

"We had to name our source," said Carolina.

"How did you find out about the surprise party?" asked Mr. Parkington. "You must have been eavesdropping when I was planning it."

"You think I listened to your conversation?" asked Carolina.

"That's what eavesdropping means—to listen to people talking when they don't know you're listening," Mr. Parkington said.

"You've been spying on us!" Mr. Flapjack accused her.

"I haven't been eavesdropping," said Carolina. "I would never do that."

"Then how else could you know all these things?" Mr. Flapjack asked.

Skits and I were too far away to hear their conversation. At that point I thought they were excited about our paper.

"Hello!" I called, walking up to them. "I suppose you're all here for autographs? Or in my case, *paw*tographs."

They glared at me.

"Or . . . not?" I squeaked.

Helen met me and Skits at Carolina's. Carolina told us what the men had said. We felt awful.

"I can't believe they said it was gossip," I said. "It was all true, wasn't it?"

"'Gossip' doesn't always mean it's not true,"

said Helen. "Gossip is when you talk about other people and say things they may not want everyone to know. Usually private, or secret, stuff."

"It may or may not be true," said Carolina.

"Oh," I said. "I'm sorry I gossiped. I didn't mean to hurt anyone."

Carolina frowned. "I'm shutting down the paper after I type an apology for ruining the Parkingtons' surprise party," she said. "Tomorrow's paper will be the last."

ZOO NEWS

I still felt bad the next day. I'd ruined the surprise party. I'd gotten Mr. Flapjack in trouble. Even Ronald seemed upset.

"I'm a terrible reporter," I told Skits as we walked downtown.

Suddenly, we heard a *WEE-OOOO! WEE-OOOO!*

"A fire engine!" I said. "I bet there's an article in that."

I chased it for a few seconds. Then I stopped. "Wait," I said. "Forget it. I'm done being a reporter. We have to find something else to do."

Woof? Skits asked.

"I don't know . . . what we usually do," I said. "Walk around, sniff things, get jobs."

Next to us, a bus stopped at the light. On its side was an advertisement for the snake exhibit at the Wagstaff Zoo.

"Hey!" I said. "Let's go see that."

Skits and I ran to the zoo. Not only would we be able to see cool snakes, but we'd have a chance to see the gang too.

First we visited Jeffy the elephant. He trumpeted some alarming information.

"You saw who, Jeffy?" I asked. "Pablum and Weaselgraft?"

Talk about bad news. Those guys once opened the Perfect Pup Institute, which they claimed trained dogs to be perfect. (As if dogs aren't already perfect!) But really, Pablum was placing microchips in dogs' collars that forced them to be obedient. I busted them, but it looked like they hadn't changed.

Jeffy said he heard the men talking by his cage. "That's perfect, Pablum!" Weaselgraft had said. "We'll steal it tonight!"

"What are they planning to steal?" I asked
Jeffy. "No, don't tell me. I don't want to know."

Woof?

"No, Skits. It wouldn't be fair to repeat what
Weaselgraft and Pablum said since they didn't
know the animals were listening. That would
be eavesdropping."

Jeffy trumpeted.

"Oh. And see?" I said. "They walked away
before Jeffy could find out what they were
planning to steal. So that solves that. Now let's
go see some snakes."

I ran off a few steps. But I couldn't help myself; I ran back. "Um, which way did those bad guys walk?" I asked Jeffy.

He said they headed toward the penguins. So Skits and I did too.

"You saw them?" I asked a penguin. "What were they doing?"

The penguin said that Weaselgraft was talking about demanding a ransom. "When they give us the money, we'll be rich!" he'd said.

"A ransom?" I said. "They must be planning to steal something really valuable."

WOOF! WOOF!

"No, Skits. We can't tell Carolina," I said. "Not only would that be gossiping, but we don't even know what they're planning to steal." I talked louder, hoping the penguin could take a hint. "I WONDER WHAT IT WAS THEY WERE PLANNING TO STEAL."

The penguin honked.

"Oh," I sighed. "They walked to the tiger area before you could find out? Oh well. Let's go see those snakes, Skits."

But I went in the opposite direction.

Woof? Skits barked.

"I know the snakes are that way," I replied. "I just want to say hi to Tiger Baby first."

Skits groaned but followed me. Then Tiger Baby told us the most shocking news of all.

"They're going to steal WHAT?!" I cried.

BARKING NEWS

Skits ran in circles. *Woof! Woof! Woof!*

"You're right," I said, my heart beating fast. "We have to tell Caroli—" I stopped. "No, I can't. I don't think Carolina wants to hear anything more from me."

Woof! Woof!

"You agree? You think I shouldn't pass on this valuable tip, just because when I was

reporting before I made one little mistake?" I said.

Woof!

"*Three* little mistakes?" I repeated. "Maybe you have a point. Oh, sure, it might stop a crime, save her paper, and redeem me . . ."

Skits rolled his eyes.

Woof!

"Well, if you insist," I said. "Let's go!"

It was evening when we rang Carolina's doorbell. Nobody answered.

"Where could she be?" I asked, pacing. "I thought she was putting out one last paper tonight."

We had to tell somebody what Weaselgraft and Pablum were up to before it was too late. "Helen will know where to find Carolina!" I said.

Skits and I burst into the kitchen to find Helen eating dinner.

"WHERE'S CAROLINA?" I yelled.

"Gah!" Helen cried, splattering soup everywhere. "Don't do that!"

"We have to find Carolina—*quick!*" I said.

"She went to apologize to Mr. Parkington's sister for ruining her surprise," Helen said. "What's the matter?"

"Only the biggest story since they invented stories," I replied. "Come on, Skits!"

By the time we got to the Parkingtons' un-surprise party, Carolina had just finished apologizing to Mr. Parkington's sister.

"It's okay," said Mr. Parkington. "I told her it wasn't your fault. It was that gossiping dog. Excuse me while I get more food."

I ran over to Carolina. "Have I got a story for you!" I said. "Talk about a scoop!"

"I don't want to hear it," she said.

"But this one is true!"

"They were all true. That's why I'm in trouble."

"But—" I said.

Carolina put her fingers in her ears. "La, la, la! I'm not listening!"

It was no use.

"What are we going to do, Skits?" I asked. "We've got real news here, but she won't listen."

Woof!

"Skits," I said. "You're a genius."

THE STRANGE SNEEZE

Skits may love bones, but he's no bonehead. His plan was brilliant. Now to try it out . . .

"Attention!" I shouted to the party. "There are open auditions for *International Icon* at town hall!"

The guests froze.

"And Brian Oceanzest will be there!" I added.

With a cheer, they all bolted out the door like greyhounds after a garbage truck. They nearly knocked over Helen, who was heading up the walk.

"Helen, follow us!" I called.

We all raced to town hall. When we got there, the lights were off and the building was empty. Everyone looked confused.

Mr. Flapjack tried the door. "It's locked," he said.

"Where's Brian Oceanzest?" a woman demanded.

It was time to tell the truth.

"I'm sorry. I made that up about Brian Oceanzest," I confessed. "But I had to get

you here. A crime is going to be committed!
Thieves are going to steal the statue of General
Wagstaff and hold it for ransom."

"Looks like he's still there to me," said
Carolina, checking out the statue behind us.

"Yeah, but . . . but . . ." I sputtered.

Mr. Flapjack scowled. "Let's get back to the
party."

"Please, just wait—" I pleaded.

But they were already leaving. If I couldn't
get them to believe me, the statue would be

gone forever! Just as I was beginning to panic, a sound stopped everyone in their tracks.

AH-CHOOOOOOOOO!

Slowly, we turned to the statue.

"Hang on," said Carolina. "Since when do statues sneeze?"

"That's no statue," said Mr. Flapjack.

"That's Weaselgraft holding really, really still!" I exclaimed.

Standing on the statue's base, Weaselgraft smiled awkwardly. "Er . . . hello! Nice evening!" he said.

Behind us we heard a *CLANG*. Pablum struggled to load the real statue into his van. With all eyes on him, he let out a nervous "Hee hee."

Those two were busted . . . again!

In short order, Pablum and Weaselgraft were led away in handcuffs by the police. And who was the only paper on the scene? You guessed it! Their arrest made the front page of *Carolina's Town Crier*.

The next day, Carolina and I returned to the
statue. Lots of people were there reading our
newspaper.

"Your tip paid off, Martha," said Carolina.

"Am I your ace reporter again, Carolina?" I
asked.

"You're my *only* reporter, Martha."

"*Ace, only.* Potato, po-tah-to," I said. "Now,
about that enchilada you owe me . . ."

"You have a one-track mind, Martha,"
Carolina said.

"How many tracks do
you need?"

THE REST OF MY INTERVIEW

Q. So, Martha, did you ever get that enchilada?

A. Yes, Martha. Holy guacamole, was it worth the wait!

Q. You know, your story really could fill a book. Can't you just picture it?

A. Sure can. Maybe we could call it *Martha's Nose for News.*

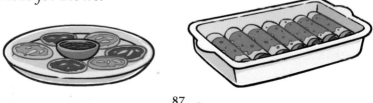

Q. Great idea! Well, I'm off to chase my tail. Thanks for the interview, Martha.

A. Anytime, Martha!

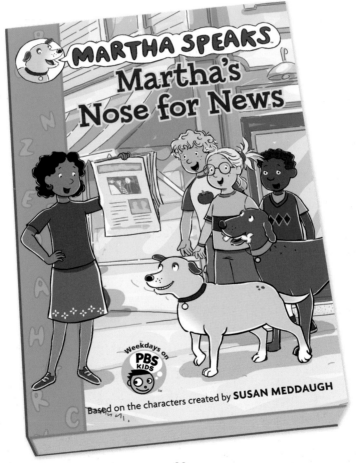

GLOSSARY

How many words do you remember from the story?

article: a story in a newspaper or magazine

deadline: the time when you need to be done with something

eavesdrop: to listen to people talking when they don't know you're listening

gossip: to talk about other people and say things they may not want everyone to know

inspect: to look at things more closely

investigate: to try to find out more about something

private: secret

research: studying, finding out facts, or learning about something

scoop: a news story no one else knows about

uncover: to find out something secret or hidden

_____'s
Town Crier

Print your own school or neighborhood newspaper!

Ask friends to be your ace reporters. Choose sections to cover, and write articles about that topic:

News: Events in your town, investigative reporting, weather.
Sports: Games and tournaments.
Arts and Entertainment: Movie and book reviews, recipes, fun facts, advice columns, birthdays, interviews with local people, and other non-news articles.
Fun Page: Comics and puzzles.

Set a deadline. After reporters have
sent their articles to you, design and print your
paper. Then deliver it to the people and dogs in
your school or neighborhood!

Martha's hot tips: Remember not to eavesdrop,
gossip, or print private information. And avoid
interviewing parrots, if you can help it.

EVERYBODY HAS A
STORY

Get the scoop on friends, family, and neighbors by interviewing them. Create a list of questions. (For more interesting replies, avoid ones that can be answered with a simple yes or no.) Who knows? Maybe you'll discover that your mom was once a roller-skating champ or your next-door neighbor is adopting a puppy. You'll be surprised at what you uncover!